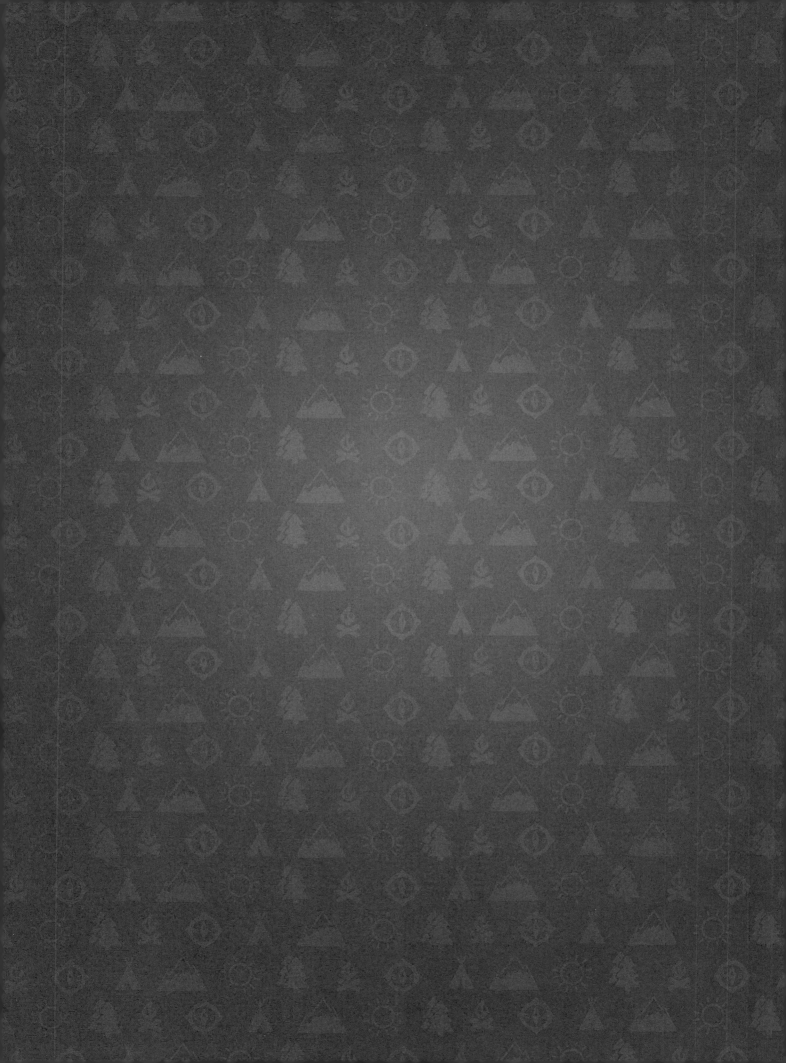

Bat in the Bunk

written by Elliot Sloyer

illustrated by Vic Guiza

Holy Moly Levi!
Best wishes for great
summer camp adventures.
Elliot Sloyer

SUMMER CAMP STORIES

Stamford, Connecticut

Library of Congress Control Number: 2014922719
ISBN: 978-0-9863743-0-2

1. Action & Adventure – Fiction   2. Camping & Outdoors – Fiction
3. Friendship – Fiction   4. Mammals – Fiction

Visit us on the web: www.summercampstories.com

Production Date: March 2015
Printed by Guangzhou Yi Cai Printing, Guangzhou City, China
Job/Batch#: 4381-0

Four Colour Print Group, Louisville, Kentucky, United States
First Edition

35 Toilsome Brook Rd.
Stamford, CT 06905
United States

Design and text layout by Margaret Cogswell
www.spiderbuddydesigns.com

To my wife, Diane, and our campers, Rebecca, Coby and Zimi -
thanks for all the joy!

E.S.

To my wife, Michelle, for being the engine of my life; and to my
daughters, Sandra and Katherine, who are the oil in my engine.

V.G.

It was a beautiful day in Tannersville, Pennsylvania, as Rafi, the camp driver, steered the bus towards Camp Massad. The birds were singing, the tadpoles were swimming, and the empty bunks were eagerly awaiting the arrival of excited campers.

In the back of the bus, David and Elliot were catching up on everything that happened since last summer. Three years earlier, they met for the first time at camp. They instantly became great friends and always looked forward to reuniting on the camp bus.

As everybody piled out of the bus, they joyfully inhaled the cool, crisp, mountain air.

David ran into the camp doctor, Dr. Romanowitz, who had taken care of him last summer when he didn't feel well. They walked to the infirmary to give David's asthma medicine to the nurse for safekeeping.

Elliot caught up with his friend, Emily. She lived in Alaska during the school year, which Elliot thought was pretty cool. Emily was the only person he knew who did not live in the continental United States.

As Elliot and Emily walked to their bunks, Elliot felt a familiar pain in his stomach. He felt it on the first day of camp every summer. It was like a bad stomachache, but Elliot knew it wasn't caused by anything he ate. "Are you feeling okay?" Emily queried.

"Yeah, I feel good," Elliot responded shyly, "why do you ask?"

"It's just that your face looks a bit pale, and you're holding your stomach," Emily replied.

DON'T WALK IN FRONT OF ME,
I MAY NOT FOLLOW.
DON'T WALK BEHIND ME,
I MAY NOT LEAD.
JUST WALK BESIDE ME AND
BE MY FRIEND.   A. Camus

"Well, actually I don't feel that great," Elliot admitted. "My stomach hurts and I feel a little nauseous. I've felt this same pain in my stomach the first few days of camp every summer. I was sure this year would be different, but I think I'm a little homesick again. I kind of miss my parents, my dog, Rusty, and all my friends back home in Stamford."

THE BEST WAY TO CHEER YOURSELF UP IS TO CHEER SOMEBODY ELSE UP
M. TWAIN

"Wow! I know exactly how you feel," Emily said. "Even though I love camp, at the beginning of every summer I always miss my mom, my little sister, Olivia, and my dog, Tuki. Three years ago I actually cried on my first day at camp, but as soon as I made friends I felt a lot better. Now I bring my favorite stuffed animal, Boo-Bah, with me to camp, and that makes me feel like I'm home."

"I know I'll feel a lot better in a few days once we start doing fun stuff," Elliot said.

"I have an idea," Emily suggested. "Let's meet at the lake later and try to catch salamanders!"

"Sounds great," Elliot replied, "I'll meet you there after I unpack my bags."

This summer David and Elliot's counselor was Joel.
Rumor had it Joel was the best counselor in camp.

He taught everybody
how to play sports,

how to swim,

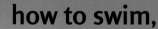

and even how to
pitch a tent.

Joel made sure to keep all the campers busy
so that they forgot about missing home.

Every night, before leaving the bunk to
hang out with the other counselors, Joel
had a fun routine. He would say good night
to each camper in any language they chose.
Joel was in college, studying to be a linguist, so he spoke
a lot of different languages. You could never stump Joel;
it seemed like he spoke every language on the planet!

BONSOIR!

"French, please," Claude called out first.

"Bonsoir, Claude," Joel replied.

"Japanese!" Jack shouted from across the bunk.

"Oyasumi," Joel responded.

OYASUMI!

¡BUENAS NOCHES!

"Mexican, please," David said.

"Mexican is not a language," Joel explained. "Mexico is a country, and the people who live there are Mexicans. But people in Mexico speak Spanish, so 'buenas noches' to you, David."

"Swahili," Andrew chimed in.

"Lala Salama, Andrew," Joel said.

"Italian, please!" Harry shouted from the top of his bunk bed.

"Buona notte," Joel responded.

Just then, Rebecca, the camp mother, walked into the bunk. Rebecca was a great camp mother. She always made sure that everybody at camp felt safe and happy, just like your mom would at home.

"People, listen up," Rebecca said, "I have a quick announcement. We have a new night watchman this summer, and his name is Shomair. If you ever need anything after Joel leaves the bunk, just call Shomair and he'll come and help you, pronto."

On her way out, Joel asked Rebecca to pick a language so that he could say good night to her too.

"Hebrew, please," Rebecca requested.

"That's easy," Joel replied. "Laila tov to you, Rebecca."

Before leaving, Joel told the bunk, "Everybody can stay up another fifteen minutes. But after that it's lights out. Remember, don't make a lot of noise because the younger campers in the bunk next door are already sleeping."

A few minutes later, David and Elliot sat on the bed playing Gin Rummy. Elliot looked up and saw something flying overhead.

At first he couldn't believe it, so he didn't say anything. Instead, he rubbed his eyes to make sure he wasn't dreaming.

Suddenly, Andrew screamed, "Holy moly, there's a bat in the bunk, there's a BAT IN THE BUNK!"

Everybody looked up in shock as a bat circled from one end of the bunk to the other. While Elliot and his bunkmates scurried to hide, they shouted at the top of their lungs, "Shomair, Shomair!"

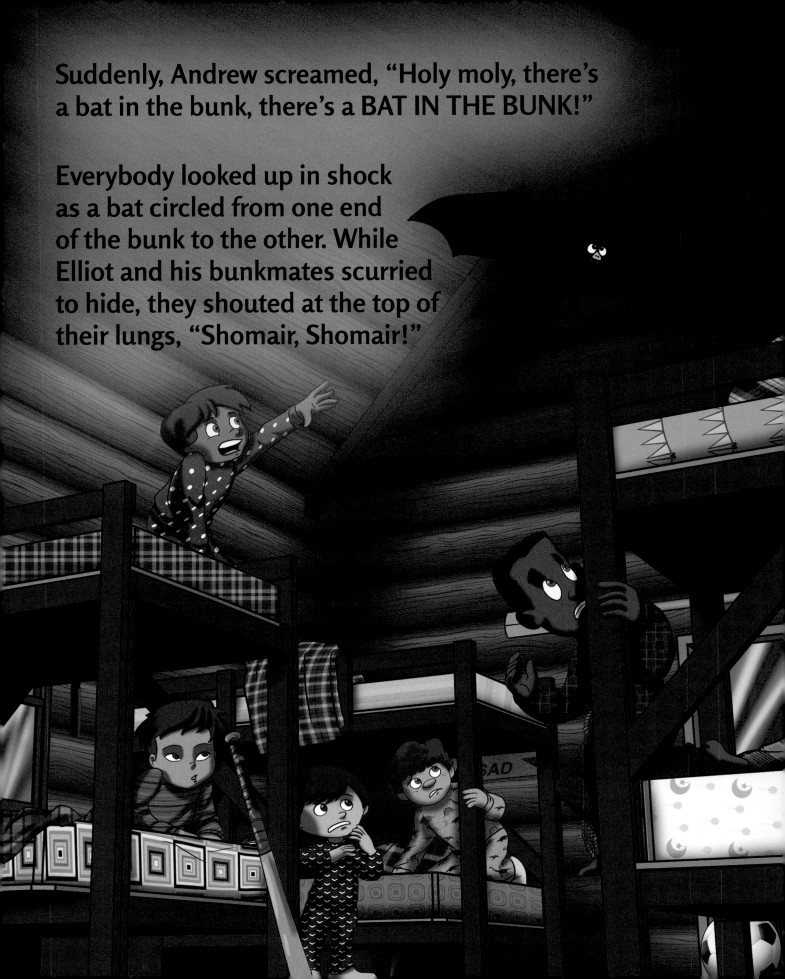

In what seemed like a few minutes, but was really only a few seconds, Shomair came crashing through the door.

"Holy cannoli! What's all the commotion about?" Shomair asked.

"There's a bat in the bunk, there's a bat in the bunk!" everybody shouted in unison.

"Well, of course there's a bat in the bunk!" Shomair exclaimed. "You guys love to play baseball. Jack even sleeps with his baseball bat."

"No, no, NO, not that kind of bat— a flying bat!" Jack screamed.

"A flying bat?!" Shomair said. "Well, why didn't you say so? I'll go find Mrs. Smart, the nature counselor."

After Shomair ran out of the bunk, Dr. Romanowitz stumbled through the door, half asleep.

"Holy rigatoni! What's all the ruckus about?"
Dr. Romanowitz asked.

"There's a bat in the bunk, there's a bat in the bunk!"
everybody shouted in unison.

"Well, of course there's a bat in the bunk!"
Dr. Romanowitz exclaimed. "You guys love to
play baseball. Claude even sleeps with his
baseball mitt."

WHO IS WISE? ONE WHO LEARNS
FROM EVERY PERSON
Ethics of the Fathers 4:1

"No, no, NO, not that kind of bat— a flying bat!"
Claude screamed.

"A flying bat?!" Dr. Romanowitz said. "Well, why didn't
you say so? I'll try to find Mrs. Smart right away."

After Dr. Romanowitz left, Rebecca marched through the door.

"Holy minestrone! What's all this mayhem about?" Rebecca asked.

"There's a bat in the bunk, there's a bat in the bunk!" everybody shouted in unison.

"Well, of course there's a bat in the bunk!" Rebecca exclaimed. "You guys love to play baseball. Harry even sleeps with his baseball cleats."

"No, no, NO, not that kind of bat— a flying bat!" Harry screamed.

"A flying bat?!" Rebecca said. "Well, why didn't you say so? I'll go find Mrs. Smart."

A few minutes after Rebecca left the bunk, Joel came rushing through the door.

"Holy pepperoni! What's all this pandemonium about?" Joel asked. "You guys were supposed to be asleep an hour ago."

"There's a bat in the bunk, there's a bat in the bunk!" everybody shouted in unison.

"Well, of course there's a bat in the bunk!" Joel exclaimed. "You guys love to play baseball. David even sleeps with his baseball cap."

"No, no, NO, not that kind of bat— a flying bat!" David screamed.

"A flying bat?!" Joel said. "Well, why didn't you say so? I'll go find Mrs. Smart."

Before Joel could leave, Mrs. Smart, Dr. Romanowitz, Shomair, and Rebecca stampeded through the door.

"So, where is this flying bat that everybody is talking about?" Mrs. Smart asked.

In all the hoopla, nobody saw where the bat actually went.

"Well, if the bat isn't flying around, it must be resting somewhere in the bunk," Mrs. Smart surmised.

So, Mrs. Smart and all the grown-ups began searching for the flying mammal. First, they scouted the cubby room, but they couldn't find the bat.

Then they searched the bathroom, but didn't see any sign of the bat. As they marched into the showers, Mrs. Smart suddenly stopped in her tracks.

"Holy guacamole!" Mrs. Smart said.

"Do you see the bat?" Dr. Romanowitz asked.

"No, but I see how the bat probably got into the bunk,"
Mrs. Smart replied. "Take a look at the tear in that screen.
I bet the bat flew in through that hole."

VISION
IS THE ART OF
SEEING THINGS
INVISIBLE

J. Swift

As tension in the bunk grew, the grown-ups shuffled into the closet, determined to find the intruder. Just then, David noticed the bat resting on the shelf next to his bed. He was so scared he could barely move, but he quickly came up with a plan.

Cautiously, David grabbed his fishing net next to his bed. He counted to five in his head as he worked up the courage to try to catch the bat.

One... two... three... four... five...

YOU MISS 100% OF THE SHOTS YOU DON'T TAKE
W. Gretzky

David swung the net over his head, but the bat swooped away too quickly. David instantly rolled off his bed and zigzagged across the bunk, following the bat's frantic escape. With one final lunge, David caught the bat safely in his net.

"Eureka," David shouted, "I caught the bat, I caught the bat!"

Mrs. Smart raced in to see what just happened. She carefully put the bat in a jar and let everyone take a look at it. Mrs. Smart explained that bats play an important part in nature and don't want to bother people, but sometimes they accidentally fly indoors and don't know how to get back outside.

Later, Mrs. Smart took the bat outside and set it free. Nobody slept very well that night, but everyone was glad that the bat was no longer in the bunk. The bat was happy, too.

The next morning the whole camp was talking about the bat in the bunk, and how brave David was to catch it by himself.

After breakfast, Emily and Elliot sat on a bench together. While Emily made a lanyard, Elliot wrote a letter home.

July 12

Dear Mom & Dad and Rusty,

When I got here last week my stomach really hurt a lot, but I didn't go to the infirmary. I realized I was just a little homesick again. I was talking to my friend, Emily, (you remember Emily, you met her on visiting day last summer) and she was homesick too. We ended up going to the lake to catch salamanders together. That was a lot of fun!

My counselor is Joel. He is very nice. He says good night to us in any language we want. Last night I chose Pig Latin, which is "oodgay ightnay." Tonight I'm going to choose Chinese. I'll let you know how to say it.

You probably won't believe me, but last night there was a bat in our bunk— for real! NOT a baseball bat, but a real flying bat! Even though all the grown-ups searched for the bat, David ended up catching it with his fishing net. Then we all got to look at it. It was really cool! Mrs. Smart let it go outside. Today, Haskel the handyman is fixing the screen where the bat flew into the bunk so it won't happen again.

On trip day we are going to Gabel's for ice cream and then to Dorney Park. Joel and all of my bunkmates are going to ride every roller coaster together 100 times. I have a feeling this is going to be the greatest summer ever!

Love,
Elliot

P.S. I think Emily "likes" me.

Campers of the Year

Goldstein

Frenkel

Kaminski

Abramov

Rabbi Deb

Pitkoff

Rudy

Wahba

Lilienfeld

Shapiro

Halperin

Metzger

Schwartz

Charnoff

Schlakman

Alexander

Israel

Rosenfeld

Fischler

Seidemann

Soclof

Perlin

Haron

Dusi

Miles

Rimerman

Weiss

Avi Biran Judaica

Linzer

Doueck

Jankelovits

Vayner

Maron